Mary L. Meaney

Cottage evening Tales, for young People

Mary L. Meaney

Cottage evening Tales, for young People

ISBN/EAN: 9783337024420

Printed in Europe, USA, Canada, Australia, Japan

Cover: Foto ©Andreas Hilbeck / pixelio.de

More available books at **www.hansebooks.com**

Cottage Evening Tales,

███████████████████████████

FOR YOUNG PEOPLE.

COMPILED

BY THE AUTHOR OF "GRACE MORTON."

PHILADELPHIA:

PETER F. CUNNINGHAM, Catholic Bookseller,

No. 216 North Third Street.

1865.

Cottage Evening Tales

IN the small village of L— was a neat little school house, built of stone. Over the porch clustered in sweet profusion roses and sweet brier. On one side was a playground, and on the other a large beautiful garden in which stood the cottage of Miss Onslow, to whom the school belonged. She was well qualified for the important task of instructing those committed to her care, since she not only taught them worldly learning, but also planted the seeds of piety and virtue in their hearts. She was universally beloved.

One morning the inhabitants of the usually quiet village were considerably excited by the arrival of a traveling carriage, drawn by four horses. It contained a lady dressed in deep mourning, a little girl and female attendant, and halted at the door of the school. The pupils all threw down their books, and in spite of the commands of Miss Onslow rushed to the windows to gaze at the extraordinary sight, for a carriage drawn by four white horses had never before been seen in that secluded place.

Miss Onslow went out to salute the stranger, who inquired if there was a cottage to be rented in the village. The teacher replied that she wished to rent her own, which she pointed out; the lady soon proved that she was both respectable and independent, and the terms were quickly settled. She took possession next day, Miss Onslow removing to the school, which suited her best as a residence. Mrs. Grenville (so was the stranger named) soon became a favorite, and her little daughter, Nina, won every heart by her piety and modesty. . Miss Onslow found the lady a great acquisition, and they soon became inseparable.

"I am very fond of children," said Mrs. Grenville one day, "and I think we might both amuse and instruct them by having Saturday Evening conversations, on subjects connected with religion and morality. I will give one every other Saturday, and you shall give the others."

Her friend was delighted with the idea, and the next Saturday was appointed.

First Evening.

"Bear with one another."

A LARGE number of children assembled at the cottage at the appointed hour in eager anticipation of the pleasure awaiting them. Mrs. Grenville, turning to Mary Day, who had just entered, asked why her brother had not come with her.

"Oh, he would not come because we had quarrelled—I thought him very unreasonable—only think of his accusing me of stealing his marbles—of being sulky and disobliging, because I do not want to play at his boisterous games. His behaviour to me was perfectly shocking, and I did not care much to come with him—but what are you going to discourse about this evening?"

"You have furnished us with a very good subject, dear Mary, and I will relate the history of two little friends of mine, which, I trust will benefit you, by showing the fault you have just committed towards your brother:

"Josephine was about ten years old, and her brother Charles nearly seven. Both were intelligent—were generally obedient to their parents, and might be termed good children, but Charles had lately become very self-willed and overbearing in his intercourse with his sister, and she had contracted the habit of speaking of his faults to whomsoever she met, without necessity. What would *you* call *that* habit, Mary?"

"I believe you would call it detrac-
tion," she replied, blushing, whilst a
tear trembled in her eye.

"You are right, my love; but, to
continue my story, it is true those were
great faults in Charles, but still his
faults did not excuse hers. Their uncle
had lately returned from the East Indies,
and came to spend some months with
them. He was in very bad health, and
rather peevish when there was much
noise or bustle, but he was exceedingly
fond of children and very kind to them,
though he never weakly indulged them.
Now the constant contention between
his nephew and niece so greatly annoyed
him, and he resolved to endeavor to
cure them both, for their own sakes as
well as for his own. One morning he
told them he intended to spend the next
day with a friend, who was to have a

sailing party on the lake, near his own house, and that he would take them with him. They were very much.delighted, for they seldom had such an invitation.

"A few hours afterwards Josephine rushed into her uncle's room weeping bitterly, and said that Charles had behaved in the most outrageous manner, and had broken her doll, because she had refused to put it aside to play ball with him, and that it was always some such scene when she did not do exactly as he choose—in short she had no pleasure in his company.

" 'I hope, dear uncle,' she continued, 'you will not take him with you to-morrow, for he will spoil all our pleasure.'

"Her uncle made no reply, but looking suddenly at his watch exclaimed : 'I had nearly forgotten to send away this letter," and left the room.

"Soon afterwards Charles entered in search of a book, and not seeing his uncle, who was reclining on a sofa, exclaimed: 'Josephine is so cross and disobliging that, if my uncle takes her with him to-morrow, I do not much care about going. She will be telling everybody I am *this* and *that*. I hope she will say she is sorry, for after all I don't like to quarrel with her: yet, why cannot she play with me in the way I ask her?' He left the room muttering that she would spoil all his pleasure if she went with his uncle.

"The next morning the two children were bustling about at an early hour, and appeared at the breakfast table dressed in their best. Their uncle came in and remarked to their mother, that, as the day was so beautiful, he should have a delightful ride to his friend's on horseback.

" 'On horseback!' exclaimed Josephine, 'Who then will drive us?'

" 'I am going alone,' he replied, and, to avoid any explanation, he bid their mother good morning, and departed.

" The children were speechless from astonishment, and turning an inquiring look towards their mother, she also left the room without noticing them, and they remained alone. They had not spoken to each other since their quarrel, poor children, they had not reflected that if they had died that night, they were at warfare with each other. Their parents knew of the whole affair, but at the request of her brother had not interfered.

" They sat and looked at each other for some time: at length Josephine said, 'It is all your fault Charles, that we are left at home—my uncle is, no doubt, displeased at your conduct yesterday.'

" 'How did he know it, and why did he not then take you?' asked her brother.

" To this she made no answer.

" 'Well, then,' continued Charles, 'if such be the case let us resolve never to quarrel again.'

" 'If you would not be so headstrong and impatient we should never disagree,' replied his sister.

" 'And if you would not be always telling my faults, I should never be angry with you for more than a minute,' replied Charles, for he was really good-hearted.

" They embraced each other with many promises of never quarreling again.

" Their uncle returned to supper, and related the delightful party on the water. a pony race, and other varieties, but

never even glanced towards the discon-
solate children. At length Charles
rushed up to him, and sobbing bitterly,
said, 'What have we done, dear uncle,
that you broke your promise to take us
with you, and will not even now speak
to us ?'

"The good old gentleman told them
how he knew of their disagreement, and
explained how sinful it was to quarrel;
then how wrong it was in Josephine to
relate the faults of her brother, keeping
back her own. 'I am sure,' continued
he, 'that had you given Charles an obliging answer, and a good reason for not
playing as he wished at that moment,
he would not have been so unreasonable.
You have no right to repeat his faults,
and thus injure him in the estimation of
another, unless with fraternal charity
you speak of them to those who have

charge over him for his good. A pious
writer says : 'If thy intentions be good,
and thou really mean to correct the fault
of thy brother, begin by correcting thy
own.' Was that your intention when
you complained to me of his conduct
yesterday ?'

" Josephine hung her head and burst
into tears.

"'And you, dear Charles,' continued
the old gentleman, 'learn to give up
your own will and condescend to that
of others, and remember, that if we are
not willing to suffer anything from
others, if we give way to our temper and
ill humor upon the slightest provocation,
how can we call ourselves the followers
of Him who, when He was reviled, did
not revile; when He suffered, threatened
not? Ask pardon of God and of each
other for your faults, and if, during a

month, you can refrain from similar
ones, I shall be rewarded for the pain I
have suffered in thus having been obliged
to punish you for your good.'

"The children embraced each other,
and from that day were inseparable;
the one became patient, docile and self-
denying; the other charitable, meek
and obliging."

This story made a deep impression on
Mary Day, and when she went home
she asked her brother's pardon, and
after struggling with her evil propensity
of talking of the faults of others, she
was heard to thank God, that, through
Mrs. Grenville, she had learned to know
herself.

Second Evening.

"**Always Tell the Truth.**"

GOOD evening, my dear child-dren," said Miss Onslow, "shall I select a subject for the evening, or will one of you do so?"

A little boy advanced and whispered something to her.

"Very well," she replied, "you shall tell the story, Eugene."

The child blushed, but, without hesitation, commenced as follows:

"The story I am going to tell you relates to those children, who, when they do mischief, try to excuse themselves by laying the fault on others. There were four children, named Margaret, Nancy, Janette, and Robert, and they all had the fault I have spoken of. One day their mother went out to dine with a friend, and said she hoped they would behave well in her absence, and not give the nurse unnecessary trouble. For a little while all went on very well, but the nurse having left the room on an errand, Robert broke the window-glass with his ball—Nancy scorched a new frock, just made for her by her mother, by holding it too near the stove whilst warming it to wrap her doll in—in short, when their mother returned the room was in complete confusion.

"'Who broke the window?' said she.

"'It was not I,' they all exclaimed, except Robert, who said, 'It might have been one of the girls.'

"'Well,' replied their mother, 'I shall ask your guardian angels not to let you go to sleep to-night, unless I am told who did the mischief.''

"The nurse then brought the scorched frock, and remarked that she could not imagine how it had become so. Nancy had replaced it in the drawer from whence she had taken it.

"'Who did this?' inquired the mother, glancing at each of the children.

"Janette said that Nancy was always holding things to the fire, and the latter retorted that she and Margaret did the same. Each one laid the blame on the other, but each concealed the truth, not only regarding the pieces of mischief spoken of, but many other things their mother inquired into.

"The next morning their excellent parent inquired how they had rested the night before.

" 'I could not sleep at all,' said Robert.

" 'Nor I,' remarked Nancy; indeed they had all been kept awake by conscience.

" 'Do you really mean to say,' inquired Robert, 'that my gurdian angel kept me awake because—'

" 'Because you broke the window? Yes, my dear child, your guardian angel whispered to you how sinful it was to disguise the truth, and try to lay the blame on another. And did he not whisper to you, Nancy, that you scorched the frock, and wished Margaret or Janette to bear the blame? I will tell you a circumstance that happened when I was a child. I was playing in the drawing-room with my brothers and sisters, and we were not allowed to play there. You see that was an act of disobedience.

One of my brothers struck his ball against a large mirror, and, without injuring the glass, it fell upon an inkstand on the marble slab beneath, upset the ink, which covered the marble and spoiled several books. We were very much frightened, and instead of running at once to our mother and telling what we had done, we covered it over with the books. Some days afterwards my mother discovered the slab completely spoiled with the ink. On being questioned we all denied having done it, except my brother, who had been the offender—he skulked out of the room to avoid being questioned. I was thought to have done it, as I was very heedless. I would not tell on my brother, neither would the others, so I was punished, and he saw me punished for his fault without having courage enough to own

that he had done the mischief; though
we were all to blame for playing there.

" 'Some months afterwards my mother
had discovered the offender, by observ-
ing that my brother's ball had a spot of
ink on it, and she then thus spoke to us
all :

" 'My dear children, what was your
motive in concealing the spilling of the
ink from me ?—See what a sin you have
committed!   You were all guilty of disobedience, in playing where I had forbidden you—you all allowed the innocent to be punished—you,' turning to
my brother, 'were the most wrong,
because you left any of your brothers or
sisters be punished for your fault—you
were all wrong, because had you told
me your brother did it, begged me to
pardon his carelessness, and owned yourselves to have been guilty of disobedi-

ence, I should probably have pardoned you all, because you told me the truth.' We never again committed that fault, and I hope my dear children that you never will.' "

"We are much obliged to you Eugene, for your story," said Miss Onslow, "and I doubt not that if any of your companions here have ever fallen into that fault, they will remember your history of this evening, and profit by it."

"But these stories are so short," said one of the children, " can you not tell us something else?" looking at Miss Onslow, and then towards Mrs. Grenville. '

"I can tell you one pretty much on the same subject," replied Mrs. Grenville: "I read it whilst in France, and will translate it for your benefit. I knew many little girls there, and this

story relates to two of them. It is called
'Sincerity Rewarded,' and commences
thus :

"'I would give you anything not to
have owned it,' said little Agnes Montfort, wiping away the tears from her
eyes, and turning from the window,
from whence she saw the family depart
on an excursion from which she was ex-
cluded.

"'Caroline is very happy now, and yet
she has no more right than myself to
enjoy this pleasure.' Thus saying she
took her books with a spiteful air, and
began to study her lessons.

"The day that Agnes made these
melancholy reflections was her birth-
day, a period looked forward to by herself, and her brothers and sisters, as a
day of pleasure. It was the month of
July, and Mrs. Montfort had promised

her children a rural feast as a reward
for their good conduct. They were to
carry provisions with them and dine in
the woods, and in the evening old Margaret was to regale them with strawberries and cream in her hut. It was a
beautiful day, when an act of disobedience in the part of Agnes deprived
her of sharing in it.

"On the evening before Mrs. Montfort had permitted the children to play
in a particular part of the garden, not
far from which was a green house filled
with rare flowers. The children had
often been forbidden to play near this
building, because they might break the
glass windows, and perhaps destroy the
precious plants it contained. After
watering their little gardens, Agnes
proposed to Caroline to play at battledore in the meadow, but finding that

place occupied by her brothers, who were playing with a balloon, Caroline proposed to go and play before the green-house, that they would have more room there, and would not be interrupted by their brothers.

"'But, my sister,' said Agnes, 'you know that mamma has often told us not to play there.'

"'Oh! I have not forgotten it,' replied Caroline, 'but she will not know it; besides the only reason for this request is for fear we should break the windows of the green house, and we will take care of that.'

"Agnes yet hesitated. At last she let herself be persuaded by her sister, who was the oldest, and the game commenced. For some time all went on very well, for the little girls were very skilful, but at length Caroline threw the shuttlecock towards the green house window. Agnes prepared to send it back with great force, but missing it she struck the window with her battledore and broke it in pieces! Frightened and confused, the girls, not daring to enter the green house to see what mischief they had done, fled to the other end of the garden.

"'Ah, what shall we do?' said Agnes, sobbing, 'and how angry mamma will be with us, she who has so often forbidbidden us to play there.'

"Caroline, who was a good little girl, was as much grieved at her sister's trouble, as by the misfortune that had happened; she tried to console her, by telling her that possibly their mother might not absorve it.

"'Oh it is very certain that she will observe it,' replied Agnes, 'and what will she think of us for concealing it, and then if she asks us, can we deny what we have done ?'

" 'No certainly not,' replied Caroline, 'but she will be occupied about the feast, and really she will not see the misfortune that has happened to us.'

" Agnes felt that she acted wrongly in not owning immediately the fault she had committed; but the fear of being deprived of the pleasures of the next day, stifled her good sentiments and she resolved not to tell her mother, hoping that the accident would not be discovered that day.

" The next morning the children rose sooner than usual, and at ten o'clock they were all assembled in the parlor, where they awaited their mother. In the midst of the joy and bustle of the morning, Agnes and Caroline had forgotten the accident of the previous evening, but, seeing their mother enter with a grave look, they recollected their fault, and guessed that she had discovered it.

"'My children,' said Mrs. Montfort, 'I went this morning to gather a bouquet of rare flowers to present to Agnes, whose feast day it is, and I have found one of the windows broken in the greenhouse. As I have often forbidden you to play there, I can scarcely believe you disobeyed me, yet before I question the gardener on the subject, I desire to know if any of you have been guilty of it?'

"'It was not I, mamma,' exclaimed all the children except Agnes and Caroline.

"Mrs. Montfort remarked it, and addressed her oldest daughter: 'you do not answer, Caroline? I hope, however, that at your age you are incapable of disobeying your mother, and I have too good an opinion of you to believe it; but answer me sincerely, did you break the window?'

"Caroline at first intended to tell the truth when her mother questioned her, but the shame of showing herself unworthy of the confidence placed in her, prevailed over her more upright sentiments, and she replied almost without hesitation : 'No, mamma.'

"Her eyes cast down, and her heart beating, Agnes awaited the terrible question; after a moment's silence her mother turning to her said: 'Can it be you, my dear Agnes?' From the affectionate tone with which Mrs. Montfort made this inquiry one would have said that, without breaking the truth, she expected Agnes to say *no*.

"Agnes was almost tempted to follow the example of her sister, and by an evasive reply get rid of any further question, but thought that a lie would offend God, whom she had been taught to revere, conquered all others, and bursting into tears, she exclaimed: 'Yes, mamma, I have been guilty enough to disobey you, and I did break the window.'

"Mrs. Montfort appeared extremely affected on hearing these words, and said very sadly, 'Agnes, I am very much grieved to be obliged to punish you on your feast day, this day that I expected to see you so happy! But the reason is still more grevious. Disobedience is a grave fault, and when it is not repressed may cause such serious misfortune to children, that I should act against my duty if I hesitated to show my displeasure. I am sorry that I cannot permit

you to take part in the pleasures of to-
day. Retire to your study-room and
learn your lessions as usual; your brothers and sisters will follow me to the
country, since they have done nothing
to merit punishment.'

"On hearing this sentence, the heart
of poor Agnes was nearly broken with
grief, but she did not dare to murmur.
Caroline who well knew that she deserv-
ed to partake her sister's punishment,
but who had not courage to avow her
fault, begged her mother, with tears, to
pardon Agnes. The other children
joined their entreaties, (for Agnes was
loved by them all,) and offered to pay
for the broken window with their own
money. Mrs. Montfort was inflexible;
she repeated that it was very painful to
punish Agnes, but that her duty required it. Seeing that all their en-

treaties were useless, the children ceased to importune her, and poor Agnes retired to her study-room. She ran to the window and saw the whole party leave the house; but for her carelessness she would have been with them, and it was when they were out of sight that she involuntarily exclaimed: 'I would give anything not to have owned it!'

"She even thought it was doubly unjust to punish her so severely, whilst her sister, who had partaken her fault of disobedience, and had also added a lie to that fault, was caressed and rewarded.

"After having wept a long time, and given free course to her spiteful and sad thoughts that agitated her, she at length began to reflect, and called to mind all she had heard repeated on the necessity of being sincere, and the baseness attached to falsehood. She began to think that in fact she had told the truth, and consequently fulfilled part of her duty. This reflection calmed her in a sudden and extraordinary manner; soon she began to study her lessons, dried her tears, and attended to her duties with courage and even with pleasure. So true it is that the consciousness of having acted uprightly, even under trying circumstances, is sufficient to recall calm and serenity to the heart.

"Thus occupied, the time passed rapidly away, and before Agnes observed that it was already evening she heard the laugh of her young brothers.— Knowing by this that the party had returned, she quitted the study-room and went to meet them, and without complaining of her punishment, listened with great interest to the recital of their pleasures.

"A short time after this Mr. Evelyn, the father of Mrs. Montfort, proposed to give a feast to his grand children and their friends, and he announced, at the same time, that the young boy and girl who should have given the best proofs of good conduct during the three pre- ceeding months, would be named King and Queen of the feast.

"It was to take place in fifteen days, and during all that time not the least fault was committed by the young pre- tenders, so ambitious were they of the promised honor. The day expected with so much impatience at last arrived. The children assembled, as well as some friends of the family, who were invited to decide on the merits of the candidates.

"After having carefully examined the conduct of each, Edward Vivian, a boy of ten years old, whose parents resided in the neighborhood, and were intimate with the Montfort family, was unanimously elected King,, amidst the applause of the assembly. The honor of being Queen balanced for some time between Caroline and Agnes Montfort, whose conduct was generally exemplary, but at last it was decided in favor of Caroline, because of the fault committed by Agnes on the evening before her birth-day.

"Seeing herself thus punished a second time for a fault of which her sister was equally guilty, Agnes could not, without great effort, prevent herself from exclaiming against the injustice of this choice. But as she tenderly loved her sister, who had at the time been sincerely grieved at her disgrace, the generous girl contained herself and kept silence, The crown of white roses, the sign of royalty on this occasion, was about to be placed on the head of Caroline, when a gentleman in the company rose, and making a sign to prevent the crowning of the young Queen, asked to be heard.

"'I am truly grieved, Madam,' said he, addressing Mrs. Montfort, 'to be obliged to divulge the faults of my young friends, and still more of those whose good conduct is so remarkable—I mean that of your daughters; but the magnanimity of one of them deserves to be rewarded. I happened to be witness of the breaking of the green-house window—I was walking in the grove unperceived by the young ladies, I overheard the conversation in which Caroline persuaded her sister to go and play there, and the resistance that Agnes at first made to this proposal. It is true that the battledore of Agnes broke the glass, but it was in consequence of Caroline having thrown the shuttlecock so near the window that the accident must necessarily happen. The fault was equal on both sides.— Agnes alone had the courage to own her fault, and the virtue to be silent on that of her sister. She has already been punished for her disobedience; permit her now to receive the reward of her sincerity. Her upright and good heart has preferred to endure a personal mortification rather than reveal the share her sister had in her fault, and it is to reward such generosity that I now deprive Caroline of the honor you had decreed for her.'

"All the assembly listened to this recital with as much surprise as admiration; whilst the unhappy Caroline, overwhelmed with confusion, retired from the circle, where she had triumphantly advanced to receive the crown. Mrs. Montfort, although enchanted at the generous conduct of Agnes, was deeply grieved to find her eldest daughter capable of such duplicity. She thanked her friend, and calling Caroline to her, said:

"'I think, my daughter, that it is not necessary to represent to you the consequences of dissimulation, for I see how much you feel the mortification to which your conduct exposes you. But, however painful it may be to blush before your friends, the pain is nothing compared to that which you should feel for having committed such a fault in the sight of the Almighty. Ask pardon of Him on your knees for such an offence. I impose no punishment on you, unhappy child; pursuaded that your conscience, and the contempt of your friends are more painful than any chastisement I could inflict. May this terrible lesson be useful to you, and learn, my children, that a fault, however well concealed it may be, is sooner or later discovered.'

"Mrs. Montfort left the room, and returning a few minutes afterwards, took Agnes in her arms and tenderly embraced her, saying: 'I cannot express to you, my dear child, the pleasure your conduct has given me. You understand now so perfectly the advantages which result from a strict adherence to the truth, that I need not repeat them. Preserve, my love, the same integrity in all the actions of your life, and in being happy you will make others so, and become an ornament to society.'

"She then took the crown of roses

and proclaimed Agnes the queen of the feast, and fastened around her waist a blue ribbon, on which her name was hastily but distinctly embroidered.

"The day passed in pleasure, and Caroline felt her grief lessen, as she witnessed the efforts of her little sister to dissipate her melancholy. I will only add that Agnes became as amiable a woman as she had been a child, and Caroline, never forgetting the terrible lesson, became, like her sister, a model of goodness..

On this evening Miss Onslow proposed to relate some short stories which she had translated from the French, for the amusement and instruction of her little scholars. She began with the story of Annette and Richard.

"Annette and Richard were the children of a poor laborer. Having lost their parents when very young, they resolved to go to the nearest city to gain a livelihood. Richard, who was twelve years old, intended to carry messages

for those who would employ him. Annette, who was much younger, desired
also to work, but she did not know exactly in what way. It is worthy of re-
mark that in this melancholy situation
these poor children never thought of
begging their bread. An interior voice
whispered that it would be shameful to
beg, when they had youth, health and
strength. Nature frequently gives an
elevated soul and excellent heart to the
most obscure.

"Without luggage, provisions or
money, these children started for the
city. Night overtook them in the forest;
they crouched under a tree and fell
asleep in the calm of innocence and
poverty; for, after having gathered some
wild fruits to appease their hunger, they
had no other inquietude. The next
morning they had yet twenty-one miles

to go. Richard, who had slept well, felt refreshed and active, but Annette was fatigued. This last part of their journey, though most frequented, was barren and unfruitful for our little travelers. Neither fruit nor any kind of roots could they discover to refresh themselves with, and they were very hungry. Nothing would have tempted them to enter any of the houses situated on the roadside, and if they saw anybody they looked timidly at them, and continued their journey in silence.

"At last overcome by hunger, thirst and weariness, Annette began to weep; Richard consoled her as well as he could—took her on his back and carried her several miles; but, at length exhausted by his fatigue, he fell on the ground with his burden. The courageous child rose without murmuring, and again endeavored to carry his sister, but it was impossible. They were but a short distance from a beautiful castle, the owner of which, generally absent, had arrived at it about an hour before. The keeper, occupied in the different apartments, had left all the doors open; the master was walking in the garden, whilst his people were preparing an excellent repast.

"Struck by the beauty and splendid appearance of the castle, the children approached, and in gazing at this magnificent abode, partly forgot their sorrows. Seeing nobody they took courage; from the hall they entered the dining-room. There large open sideboards showed pyramids of superb fruit, sweetmeats and wines of every sort. The children remained to examine this excellent dessert, but, as self-denying as

they were honest, they did not attempt
to approach it.   Richard only wished
his sister had a little of the clear water
that sparkled in the glass pitcher.
Whilst examining these objects, so entirely new to them, they perceived near
the place where they stood, a basket
filled with rolls; Annette pushed Richard and pointed to it. He, fearing without doubt, that extreme hunger might
cause his sister to take one, seized her
by the arm and drew her from the room
—the poor little child fell fainting in
the doorway.

"But the owner of the house had followed the children without their per-
ceiving him. Witness of their delicacy
and extreme honesty, he felt interested
in them; and was thinking of the means
to be useful to them, when Annette's
accident decided him to call for help.

They soon recovered her, and the frank and simple narrative of their misfortunes made such an impression on the humane gentleman that questioned them, that he took them under his protection and provided for their welfare."

The next story was called "Michael; or, God Punishes Disobedience."

"Mathurine frequently said to her son: 'Beware, Michael, of ever taking anything from the orchard of our neighbor, Father Blaise; for the great God will punish you.'"

"Now Mathurine knew that Michael had not his equal in disobedience. She, therefore, tried to inspire him with the fear of God; for he did not fear her at all; besides, he was much oftener running in the fields than quiet at home.

"Michael did not touch the trees of Father Blaise during all that spring, and that was something gained; he did not always wait for the fruits to ripen before he ate them; they perceived that in his mother's garden the apple, pear and plum trees were stripped before their fruits were fairly grown. Michael would not, perhaps, have taken anything in his neighbor's orchard but for a peculiar circumstance. He was very fond of cherries, and there were none in his own garden, but to make amends the garden of Blaise was full of them.

"Michael passed and repassed incessantly before those large red cherries, to have the pleasure of gazing at them. What a pity to be confined to simply look at the tempting fruit!—he could easily climb the wall of the garden, stretch out his arm, then take a handful of cherries—this could be so quickly done! Father Blaise would not see him

—he would not miss. But the great God will punish him his mother has said. Bah! that is only a fable; my mother said so only to frighten me!

"Thus spoke Michael. Such is always the language of wicked children, who respect neither father nor mother; so the great God forsakes them.

"Gluttony and disobedience then drove Michael to steal the cherries of his neighbor. At the close of the day he crept along the wall, climbed it in two bounds, and was in the tree. If he had followed his first thought and taken only a handful of cherries in haste, perhaps he would have left the tree safe and sound; but to punish him, God permitted that after having remained in it a long time eating cherries, he must yet fill his pockets.

"Now, there were some sportsmen in the fields. As they were returning one

of them perceived a rabbit very near
Blaise's garden, and he shot at it. It
was exactly under the spot where Michael was. The little boy was so terri-
fied that he fell like one dead, at the
foot of the tree. Blaise, hearing the
noise, hastened to the place, thinking he
should find some game in his enclosure.
At the sight of Michael, without consciousness, he drew back; he believed
him dead. Having recovered him, he
conducted him home. The appearance
of Michael, pale and haggard, dis-
tressed his mother, but she soon understood that he had been more frightened
than hurt.

"When they were alone, Mathurine
said to her son: 'Michael, will you
ever again steal cherries from Father
Blaise ?'

" 'Oh! no, my mother," he replied;

'the great God has indeed punished me, as you have often said; I promise never again to disobey you.'

"Michael kept his word, and he did well."

Miss Onslow then related the story of "The Nuremberg Doll."

"Imagine to yourselves, dear children, a parlor somewhat in confusion; a trunk is in the middle of the room, and a lady, seated by it, draws out one article after another. This lady has just returned home. On the other side of the trunk stands a pretty little girl, with dark curly hair and rosy cheeks. Her eyes sparkle like diamonds as she gazes on the trunk with an air of expectation —she is waiting to see what her mother has brought her.

"Suddenly the mother stops and kissing her daughter, says: 'Louisa, you know a little of geography. Do you know where Nuremberg is?'

" 'Nuremberg, a city of Germany,' replied Louisa, in the tone of a parrot; 'they preserve in the church of the hospital the ornaments that are used in the coronation of Emperors; all Europe is filled with the little works of Nuremberg.' Here the roguish Louisa quitted the monotonous tone she had commenced with to give a certain emphasis to her words—'the artists are skillful in fabricating the most beautiful toys for children.'

"Here Madame de Merval interrupted her by taking from the trunk a charming little doll—not very little either—it was twelve inches in height. Its dress was black, trimmed with gold cord and bows of black satin ribbon, long sleeves down to the wrist, and a black lace cap.

A short robe over the dress was trimmed with black lace and gold flowers; on its head was a wreath of gold flowers that trembled at every movement.

" Oh, how joyfully Louisa thanked her mother for such a charming doll.

" 'I wish, Louisa,' said Madame de Merval, as she placed it in her hand, 'I wish this doll to stand always on the mantel-piece by the side of your bed; she is named like yourself; you will look at her every morning and evening; you will consult her, for she is a good counsellor; she is not curious, and always says her prayers. You will be careful not to take her off the stand, for she would no longer be pretty.'

" At this moment the doll extended her arms, folded them together, and made such a pretty salutation to Louisa that she was near letting her fall, through astonishment.

"'Well, Louisa, you admired just now only her beauty; you see that there is something better than that in her—talent and goodness. She is your little friend, and yet you will not always love her, because she will tell you the truth without disguise.'

"Louisa carried the precious doll to her chamber, and looked at her until night. She expected another salutation, but the doll did not make it until Louisa was in bed. She soon fell asleep, and did not awaken until her mother came to embrace her for the last time and to look if the doll was still whole. She turned it every way, and at length placed it again by the side of Louisa's bed.

"The writer of the story goes on to say, I request my young friends to believe that I relate only what I have witnessed—for it is that only which gives a little value to this history. What would childish things, invented by myself, be worth? Besides, I am incapable of it. Thus I shall not, on my own authority, say that Louisa, good and amiable otherwise, sometimes forgot her prayers or her reading, and had an extreme curiosity; these would be calumnies from which I should guard myself. I should neither have any merit in saying, without it was so, that the name of Louisa had degenerated into a genteel diminutive, and that generally she was called Loulou. They called her Loulou when she had been discreet, studious and industrious—and Madame de Merval having presented the doll as a very sensible doll, she was named Loulou. There was a learned old man, a friend of the family, who told Louisa one day that, in the Arabic language, Loulou signified pearl, and she was much pleased.

"She had then slept near her Loulou without awakening, but not without seeing her in a fine dream, which only ended at daylight with sleep. Immediately she jumped out of bed and flew towards her sister Loulou, her well-beloved. This was her first thought, but—wonderful! Behold, Loulou half closes her eyes, joins her two hands, bends and kneels, just as if she had said: 'Miss Louisa you have forgotten your prayers; you must think of God and your mother before you think of me.'

"Louisa, scarcely recovered from her astonishment, said her prayers and went to relate to her mother, in a tone of rapture, what had happened. She went to own her fault with candor; she had repaired it; and the feeling of being corrected renders one so content with one's self.

"I must, however, interrupt my story, to mention a circumstance that you have no doubt already divined. The Nuremberg doll was on springs. Madame de Merval, in passing through that city on her way to Venice, had conceived the idea of ordering the most able artizan to make a mechanical doll, of the different movements, by which lessons might be given to her child, whose faults she knew; she had wound up the doll that she might kneel, for she foresaw that Louisa would forget her prayers. There were in the pedestal as many imperceptible holes as were necessary to wind up the different movements of the doll; and you understand that Madame de Merval had only to come every evening, and having observed the conduct of Louisa during the day, wind up the springs. She had been constrained to

adopt this means of correcting her
daughter, as if the words of a tender
mother ought not to be more powerful
than anything else in the world.

" The day passed well, because it had
begun well; and after having contem-
plated, with admiration and a sort of respect, the graceful Loulou, Louisa went
to bed contentedly, and slept so well
that her mother could kiss without
awakening her; and it was only when
the rising sun shone on her eyelids that
she was aroused. Scarcely out of bed,
this time, she fell on her knees and
prayed with all her heart for her mother.
Children would never fail to pray for
their mother if they knew what bles-
sings their voices draw down on their
families. When she had finished, she
had her reward. Loulou was content
with her, and began to dance with joy;

and the gold flowers that covered her head trembled and glittered in the sunbeams. Louisa ran directly, out of breath, joyful and wondering, to relate the miracle to her mother, who tenderly embraced her. The day passed thus well and praiseworthily, under the influence of the Nuremberg doll. It was wonderful. Louisa was discreet, obedient; and it would have been perfect, if she had oftener thought of her books and piano.

"Now one day, as usual, the second thought of Louisa had been for her Loulou; and, looking at her very tenderly, she perceived her little fingers running, one after another, as upon the key-board of a piano. It was a fingering so light and graceful that one almost expected delightful sounds, and listened in silence. Then the hands of Loulou stopped and took out of the pocket of her dress a little book, and the doll fixed her eyes upon it as if she read attentively. Madame de Merval perceived during the day that Loulou had done her duty well, for her daughter was delightfully studious and attentive; and this result was of long duration, so that her mother was quite happy.

"But she yet desired to see Louisa cease to be curious. The little girl would search about in every direction, read in every book, and her mother had seen her listening at the doors. This is almost as odious a fault in a child as lying, because it leads to falsehoods; and then it is very unworthy, for it is an abuse of confidence. Madame de Marval resolved to punish her for it a little severely. One day she caught her reading a letter—half opening it, to see if it was an invitation to a dance—and, by the way, Louisa was punished even by her curiosity, in learning that the dance was not to be given; her mother invited two or three of her little friends to pass the day with her. You understand that Loulou was at her post. Already Louisa, the little mistress of the house, had done the honors towards her doll, by relating the fine things she did.

" 'In short, would you believe that she sees all I do; and that she dances when I do well, and gives me lessons when I do ill. She always tells the truth; she is never deceived; she divines all; she knows all.'

"Whilst Louisa was thus praising her she did not perceive that Loulou began to be animated; she stretched her neck as if to listen, and then she drew from her pocket a letter, and opening it, seemed to read. The little girls laughed outright, while Louisa said, in a low tone, 'Naughty Doll! she has not seen me do it, notwithstanding.'

"'Ah! ah! Louisa, she tells the truth —you listen, then, at doors? You read letters secretly? Oh! that is very ugly.'

"And Louisa, who had already blushed at the movements of her doll, blushed yet more at the reproaches of her companions—but this blush was not so much from repentance as from anger, and she determined to be revenged on the doll which had caused such a scene; she seized her abruptly, and without doubt, was going to break her to pieces, saying, with anger, 'It is not true, young ladies; she is a liar.' She held the doll by her head and feet, as if to break her in two, while her little friends begged

her to spare Loulou. All at once her
mother entered and looked very sternly
at Louisa, who, very much confused,
replaced the doll on the mantel-piece.

"'Ah! Louisa,' said she, 'you wished
to get rid of looks which both observed
and warned you; you could never suc-
ceed, my child, for besides the vigilant
eye of your mother, there is One above
whom your little hands could never
reach. Come here:.I wish for your only
punishment to show you what you were
going to destroy, and you will repent
and be ashamed of your anger.'

"Madame de Merval then took the
doll, opened the pedestal where the
springs were, and wound it up, 'see,
young ladies. And the springs played
charmingly, and the doll danced. The
children were delighted.

"'See, my Louisa, the secret of the

lessons given you by Loulou. It is the
work of man, where there is neither
wonder nor miracle. It was always
myself, who, after having watched your
faults through the day, recalled them to
you next morning by means of these
springs. Now I give you the key. The
doll has commenced your reformation,
but every evening wind her up, that she
may recall to you what you should avoid
in future. You listened to her rather
than to me, because you did not com-
prehend the mystery; at present it
is nothing more than play. In future,
never listen to any advice but from your
mother.'

" The mother and child embraced each
other, and the day finished joyfully."

Miss Onslow's little pupils were
delighted with this story, and repaid her
for the trouble she had taken by pro-
mising to try and profit by it.

PROCRASTINATION.

T was Mrs. Grenville's turn on this evening to relate some story. She had lately observed in her little daughter a disposition to "put off" doing anything until some other time; for her instruction, therefore, as well as of others who might have the same fault, she began as follows:

"I do not like Charlotte Morley, because she tells everything she hears," said Josephine Alton to her governess. "I should be sorry to resemble her."

"That is a very great fault in Charlotte," replied Miss Rosalie, "but before

(65)

you judge her you should remember that you have as great a fault, and—"

"And pray what is that great fault?" asked Josephine saucily, "I suppose you are harping on the old tune of 'coming directly.'"

"'And is not procrastination a great fault? Do you not lose time by not doing things at the proper moment and subject yourself and others to great inconvenience? A few days ago, for instance, your mother told you to go down to the parlor and tell a visitor she was too much indisposed to see any body, you said, 'directly, mamma,' but did not go for nearly half an hour, and the visitor had gone away much offended that nobody came to receive her.'

"'But I had forgotten what mamma said.'

"'Simply because you did not go at

the moment she told you; but amused yourself by playing on the staircase with your kitten.'

" 'Mamma, however, did not think that such a great fault '

" 'Because she has been absent from you nearly two years, and does not know you as I do; she supposed it was only from the thoughtlessness of a child; but I know, from sad experience, that it is a pernicious habit you have contracted, and which I have, as yet, vainly endeavored to correct. If you do not overcome this fault, believe me, it will finally make both yourself and others miserable.' ·

" 'Oh! Miss Rosalie, you are certainly related to the frog family—for you are always croaking;' and with this impertinent speech, the naughty child flounced out of the room.

" Mrs. Alton had but recently returned

from Italy, whither she had gone with her husband, whose declining health rendered such a change necessary; but he had died there, and she had come back, in sadness, to meet her orphan child, whom she had left under the care of her venerable grandfather and of Miss Rosalie, who was every way qualified for the important task. Josephine had fewer faults than most children of her age, (she was ten years old,) but a tendency to put off everything she was told to do had manifested itself, and considering the excellent management of her governess, it was a wonder she had not overcome such a fault. When the hour of study arrived, Miss Rosalie always took her by the hand, and led her to the school-room— If they were going to walk she gave her to understand, that if not ready-dressed at the same moment with herself, she must remain at home and study her lessons for the next day; and in everything else she pursued, the same method.— But she had lately discovered that, owing to the extreme fondness of Mr. Alton for his grand-daughter, he only smiled and humored her when she would answer 'directly, grandpapa,' without doing what was required of her; and she, therefore, resolved to acquaint Mrs. Alton with this growing fault in Josephine. Mrs. Alton saw the necessity of co-operating with her governess in the task of reforming her daughter, and after repeated trials to convince herself that it was really procrastination, and not mere forgetfulness, she agreed with Miss Rosalie as to the plan they should pursue. Old Mr. Alton had gone to spend a few months with an aged friend, and they took advantage of his absence.

"Mrs. Alton invited Charlotte to spend the day, whilst Josephine and she were playing in the garden. Miss Rosalie called the former to come immediately to her mother, who wanted her for something particular.

"'Directly, Miss Rosalie,' she replied, but continued playing with her doll.

"Half an hour afterwards, Charlotte said: 'are you not going to your mother? She will be angry at your staying so long. I never stop a moment when mother calls me.'

"'Oh! mamma never expects me to come in an instant; it is only Miss Rosalie, who is always in a flurry. I dare say I am not wanted for anything so *very* particular—however, I will go and see.'

"She soon returned pouting, and said, 'mother had wished us both to go and ride in an omnibus that was passing by, but as we did not come, and the driver would not wait, she went without us. I do believe,' she continued, 'it is all owing to Miss Rosalie, who had hurried mamma away because I said *directly*, and did not come. She said the other day I would sooner or later be punished for saying that word so often without putting it in practice. She is a mean creature to make mamma go without us.'

" ' Well,' answered Charlotte, 'I am also punished by it for I have lost a pleasant ride. You had better break yourself of that bad habit, Josephine.'

" 'Mind your own faults and do not meddle with mine,' said Josephine angrily—' I get enough schooling from Miss Rosalie. I wish grandpapa was at home, and I should have somebody to take my part.'

"The remainder of the day was spent in ill-humor on both sides. When Josephine attempted to bring on a conversation about the ride, her mother answered coldly, 'disobedience and idleness always bring their punishment.'

"The next day Miss Rosalie went to see Mrs. Morley on business, and Charlotte repeated every word Josephine had said the day before, adding, that procrastination was a dreadful defect.

"Miss Rosalie said, 'I am surprised my pupil should have uttered such expressions concerning me, and I am still more surprised, Miss Charlotte, that you should take pleasure in repeating them. It is true this is a great fault in our dear Josephine, but, at the same time, it is not more pernicious than that of repeating everything we hear.'

"'Come here, Josephine,' said Mrs.

Alton; 'your governess tells me you spoke very disrespectfully and unjustly of her to Charlotte. I am much displeased, for I have always impressed on your mind the necessity of treating Miss Rosalie with as much respect as you would your mother. I have said you spoke unjustly of her, because so far from influencing me regarding the ride, I chose to punish you, and I saw a tear in her eye at your being thus punished.'

"'But, mamma, Charlotte need not have told tales, it is a shocking habit she has. I forgot it when I spoke before her.'

"'You can see her fault, my dear child, but you do not see your own, or if you are sensible of it you let it pass without condemnation. Had you come to me the moment Miss Rosalie called you, you would have had a pleasant

ride. You would not have said all this to
Charlotte, offending your excellent in-
structress and friend—and done all this
by saying one word which expressed a
falsehood. Because when you said, I
will come directly, you did not mean to
move, nor would perhaps have come at
all if Charlotte had not reminded you
of it. It is a serious thing to offend our
parents or friends, but do you not think
it a much more serious thing to offend
God ?'

" 'Yes, mamma; but in what have I
offended God? By speaking unjustly of
my governess ?'

" 'God has appointed a time for everything; and, therefore, when you did not
obey my orders you did not fulfil the
commands of God, who requires you to
obey your parents. You came, it is true,
but it was not at the time He had ap-

pointed. Then by using that word you told a falsehood, for you did not come *directly*. You were unjust, and besides, deprived your companion of a pleasure. So you have lost time, and have disobedience, falsehood, injustice and ill-humor to accuse yourself of.'

"Josephine acknowledged her faults, and for some weeks seemed amended— but it required severe trials to cure her really and forever.

"One morning early Mrs. Alton went to spend the day at her cousin's, and told Josephine she would send for her during the day, as it was but a mile and an agreeable walk. Now it happened that Josephine did not particularly like her mother's cousin, and would rather have stayed at home, so she resolved not to hurry when she was sent for. Josephine had forgotten her late pro-

mises of obedience and resolutions to do
every thing at the appointed time; and,
therefore, she neglected to have her tasks
completed and her dress arranged at the
hour specified by her mother. About
three hours after Mrs. Alton's departure
a man on horseback rode furiously up to
the door and told Josephine she must
set out instantly for Mrs. Elwood's;
he added, 'hurry, dear Miss, for she is
much hurt,' and, without further explanation, rode off in an opposite direction.

"Josephine did not pay much attention
to his concluding words, supposing they
meant that Mrs. Elwood was hurt or displeased at her not coming with her
mother. She, therefore, according to her
old habit, loitered for an hour, and even
stopped on the road to watch butterflies
and grasshoppers. When she arrived at
Mrs. Ellwood's, she was much surprised

to find the parlor vacant, and no appearance of any one about the premises.—
There seemed to be a confusion up-
stairs, but she was too much of a stranger
to go up unannounced. At that moment, Dr. Denby alighted from his
carriage and went up the staircase.—
Poor Josephine began to feel uneasy,
and tremblingly followed him; but what
a sight met her view—her mother was
stretched on a sofa, apparently dead.

"'Oh! tell me what has happened,'
she exclaimed.

"'Your mother was thrown from the
carriage, has been insensible ever since,
and we fear will never recover,' replied
Mrs. Elwood, weeping.

"The doctor ordered every one to
leave the room, except the necessary
attendants, and Mrs. Elwood drew the
poor unhappy child from the distressing

scene. I will not attempt to describe
the grief of Josephine, or the remorse
she felt at having lingered after receiv-
ing the message. It was some time
before Mrs. Elwood understood what
had caused the accident, for in her distress she had not particularly inquired.
But when at last Josephine heard that
the axle-tree of the carriage had broken,
she exclaimed, 'I have killed my precious mother!' and in heart rending
tones, she related the following:

"'Mamma had, early this morning,
desired me to tell the coachman she had
observed a crack in the axle-tree, and to
send her word if he thought it safe
enough to go as far as Mrs. Elwood's.
I answered, ' directly, mamma,' and left
the room for that purpose; but I stopped
in the ·library to get a book I had left
there, and began to read and entirely

forgot the message. I suppose mamma
thought I had executed her orders, as
the carriage was brought to the door,
and as she did not ask the coachman
anything about it, I never thought
about it either. But did the axle-tree
really break?' she inquired eagerly, 'or
was she only thrown from the carriage
by the horses running away?'

"'The axle-tree broke whilst going
down the hill, and the horses became
frightened and upset the carriage,
throwing your mother against the stump
of a tree.'

"At that moment, Mrs. Elwood was
summoned to attend the doctor, and
Josephine was left to consider the consequence of her fault of procrastination.
After a considerable time, which was
almost insupportable to the poor child,
Mrs. Elwood came and silently conduct-

ed her to the couch of her mother, who had now recovered her faculties, but was so much bruised and her ankle sprained besides, that she would be for . some weeks a prisoner in that chamber. The doctor pronounced her out of danger, as he could not perceive there was any internal injury. Josephine fell on her knees and thanked God that her parent had not died through her fault.

"'Can you forgive me, dear mother?' she sobbed. Her mother embraced her but was not able to speak.

"Mrs. Elwood had a chapel in the house, dedicated to the Blessed Mother of God, and thither Josephine went, and throwing herself before a beautiful statue of the Holy Virgin, she prayed:—

"'Sweet Mother! I am a poor, miserable child—I have nearly caused the death of my parent by my fault—have

compassion on me, and offer the prayer
I am about to make to thy Beloved Son,
my Redeemer, that I may obtain pardon,
and grace, and strength—never again to
offend wilfully by those faults which I
have too long indulged.   Oh, my God!
Father, Son and Holy Ghost, one God!
have mercy on me, and teach me how
to walk in thy commandments.'   ¿

"Mrs. Alton recovered, and returned
home about the time that her venerable
father did.   Josephine related all that
had passed, and he only loved her the
more, now that she had no faults—at
least they were trifling ones, for she
never relapsed into her habit of procrastination, and even turned pale when
she heard the word *directly* uttered by
any one.   She was soon after permitted
to make her first communion, and became eminent for her virtues, and devo-

tion to the Blessed Virgin, whose name she also bore."

"Now, my dear little friends, I hope that any of you who are subject to the fault of procrastination, or the putting off to another moment what should be done at once, will take warning by Josephine, and, like her, ask for grace to amend a fault which will certainly make, not only yourself, but others also—wretched perhaps for life, and drive you from God."

Fifth Evening.

Industry and Obedience.

To gratify those among the children who liked *long stories*, Miss Onslow, on this evening, related the following:—

"The evening sun had just cast a last golden ray on the surrounding objects, as Mrs. Manners and her son entered a romantic pathway leading to the neighboring village. Their residence was about a mile distant, and they had only arrived the day before, having been

(83)

traveling for more than a year on account of the health of her aged father. He had departed this world as a sincere follower of the Cross, about a month previous, and she had therefore returned to her home, sad but resigned.

"She was comparing the lingering beams of the sun to the dying smiles of her venerated and Christian parent, when, as they passed a lonely cottage by the wayside, she heard sounds of lamentation. She paused, uncertain whether to inquire into the evident distress of the inmate, a feeble voice exclaimed: 'Oh, my son! where art thou? Holy Mother, protect my poor boy!' These words decided Mrs. Manners, and she entered the cottage, followed by Felix. A few kind inquiries soon unfolded the history of the widow who inhabited it.

"Her only son, who was the only

solace left her in this vale of tears, and
who was indeed her only support, had
departed early in the morning to receive
some wages due to him from a farmer
about five miles distant; he had promised to return in time to partake of
their scanty dinner; it was now nearly
night and he was yet absent. She said
that some wicked youths of the village
had tried to corrupt her beloved Felix,
and associate him in their iniquitous
courses; but he feared God, and loved
his mother, and she had never known
him to do anything that could cause
remorse or grieve her—that his love for
his parent was only surpassed by his love
for God. She knew that there was a
short route to the farmer's over a dan-
gerous and unused bridge, though persons on foot frequently went over it in
safety; and a poor idiot boy had some

hours ago entered the cottage, and whispered in her ear: 'the bridge, the bridge, beware, beware! for there are vultures waiting there! And, madam,' added she, 'I fear those wicked boys have there waylaid my child, for he would never have stayed this long without some accident.'

"Mrs. Manners said she would instantly send in search of him, and dispatched her son with orders to the steward to go with some of her people and make every possible inquiry. She desired Felix to return to the cottage after he had given his message, for she intended to remain with the widow, who was named Mrs. Truely.

"A strange sympathy drew them towards each other; both were widows, and their sons named Felix; but there was a difference between the two boys, if

Felix Truely was such as his mother described him. Felix Manners was intelligent and had a good heart, but his better qualities were obscured by idleness, selfishness, disobedience and a culpable neglect of his religious duties. Having given the necessary orders, he returned. He felt much interested in the widow and her son, and had, therefore, no inclination to disobey his mother.

"A footstep was soon after heard, and Felix Truely rushed into his mother's arms. I will not attempt to describe her joy at again beholding him. He related that the kind farmer had begged him to execute a commission, which had detained him some hours longer than he had anticipated, and had given him in return a basket of cakes, sweetmeats, and other varieties; as he left the place the idiot boy had met him and whispered, 'The bridge, the bridge!—beware, beware!' that knowing the affection of the poor unfortunate, and believing some danger to await him there, he had returned by the longer and more frequented route through the village. As he concluded his narrative, the men who had gone in search of him entered, leading in a boy whom they had found in the garden and who was weeping bitterly. Felix recognized him as one of those who had endeavored to lure him from the path of virtue, and he asked him why he wept. The boy owned that he had followed him, had seen the farmer give him the basket, and had determined to waylay and rob him of it at the bridge, which, being roofed and covered at the sides, was quite dark in many places, and he would not know who stopped him. But whilst he awaited the coming of Felix at the entrance, a horse galloped furiously on the bridge, and, dashing against him, threw him into the stream. As he could swim, he found his way to the opposite bank with some difficulty and clambered up the side of it—but, struck with his punishment and escape from death, and remorse for the crime he had meditated, he resolved to come to the cottage, own his wickedness, and resolving never again to return to his former evil ways, he begged forgiveness and their advice how to do better in the future. Mrs. Manners gave him some good advice—told him to go to the venerable priest, confess his faults with contrition and a firm purpose of amendment, without which it would avail him nothing, and be guided by him in his future course of life; and that if she heard of his perseverance in virtue, she would put him in the way to gain an honest living; for his parents were very poor, and she was willing to assist them.

" 'If your son will come to us, Mrs. Truely,' she continued, 'we will give him plenty of work, and he shall share in the instructions which I give to my Felix. You will be glad to have a companion who will set you an example of industry and obedience, my dear child,' continued she, addressing her son, who hung his head, because he too well understood her meaning.

" The proposal was accepted with gratitude by Mrs. Truely, and Felix shed tears of joy at the idea of being instructed, for he could only read and write passably, and his stock of books was very limited.

" 'I am going to the village, where I

shall remain several hours,' said Mrs. Manners one morning to her son, 'unless you are very disobedient you will not leave the house; or be idle during my absence ; and I shall expect you to know your lessons perfectly when I return. Felix Truely has already finished his work in the field, and he will study with you.'

"Felix Manners sat gazing on his books for half an hour, then rose to leave the room.

"'Where are you going ? Do you know your lessons already ?' said his companion.

"'I am going to play with Pompey, and get some peaches; I will be back presently.'

"'But your mother said we must not leave the house—pray do not go ;' but Felix was already out of hearing.

"Young Truely was so busy at his tasks that he was surprised on looking at the clock to find that his friend had been absent two hours. As he rose to go in search of him a scream from the garden smote his ear. He flew to the spot, and saw Felix struggling with a large ape, which held him by the throat. He struck it with a spade, and the animal escaped, bearing off the basket of peaches, with which the truant had intended to regale himself. As soon as the latter had recovered from his fright, his friend advised him to resume his studies as his mother would soon return, and would be grieved to find he had been so idle. 'But how did this happen?' continued he.

"'Why I heard a great chattering outside the garden wall, and opened the gate to see who it could be, when this horrible monkey flew at my basket of peaches. I would not let go—so it flew at my throat, I feel its claws yet. If Pompey had been here he would have bit him finely.'

"'Well,' replied the other, 'you see, my dear Felix, that we are always punished in some way for our faults. If you had not disobeyed your mother by going into the garden, but had studied your lesson, this would not have happened. The animal might have strangled you had not God sent me to your assistance. But come, I know my lessons and will help you to get yours. It would grieve me to see my benefactress displeased with you, and I trust you will not again act so thoughtlessly.'

"Felix was very fond of his friend and took this admonition in good part. The lessons were just completed as Mrs. Manners entered the room.

" 'I see you have not been idle to-day," said she, after Felix had recited his different tasks.

" He blushed and looked confused, but as she did not observe it, he had not moral courage or honesty enough to tell the truth or give the praise where it was due.

" One day Felix Manners said to his companion: 'I shall be ten years old on St. Felix's day, and mother has promised to give me a feast. We are to write compositions on the virtues of our patron saint, and the best one will obtain a prize; she will not tell me what the prize is to be, but I know it will be something worth having; so *mind*, I shall try hard to win it.'

" 'I hope most sincerely you may obtain it—and you certainly will, for you know I shall be a very poor rival.'

Felix Truely would not be half so much satisfied to win it himself, for he had no selfishness, and rejoiced at everything that exalted the character of the son of his benefactress.

"The day arrived and a large party assembled at Mrs. Manners' house—amongst whom was Mrs. Truely. After partaking of refreshments the two boys recited their compositions, and Felix Manners obtained the prize. An interior voice whispered that he had no right to it, but as nobody knew so but himself, save one, his selfishness got the better, and he received the congratulations of those around him. His mother told him his prize waited at the door, and he found a beautiful pony, the smallest ever seen in that neighborhood, ready saddled. His friend followed to help him to mount, but Felix could not speak, for he was ashamed of his own meanness, which we shall learn presently. After dinner another smaller prize was to be given for the best composition on any chosen subject. That of Felix Manners was a very commonplace essay on the beauties of Spring; but his companion delivered an eloquent discourse on Gratitude, in which he painted the truly Christian character of his benefactress in glowing colors. The judge awarded him the prize, which was a splendidly bound copy of the Lives of the Saints. For a moment there was a profound silence, and Felix Manners stood before his mother blushing and in tears.

"'Pardon me,' said he, 'for having received what was not justly mine. We showed our compositions to our Reverend Pastor, and he, without knowing who wrote it, pronounced my friend's decidedly the best. I knew he was a good judge, and I was so disturbed at the idea of not succeeding, that Felix Truely offered me his, if I thought it would obtain the preference. He said he would not recite his, if he supposed it could win the premium from his dear Felix. I was mean and selfish enough to accept it; the pony is therefore his, and his generosity and friendship have opened my eyes to those faults by which I have so often offended God, and grieved the best of mothers.'

"Mrs. Manners embraced her son, and thanked God for having touched the heart of her beloved one, and a pressure of the hand told her gratitude to Felix Truely.

"But a terrible storm was ready to burst over the head of the latter; showing that our life shall not always be sunshine, 'for whom the Lord loveth he chastiseth, and scourgeth every son whom he receiveth.' The overseer of the farm disliked Felix because he could not corrupt him, for he was an unfaithful servant, though Mrs. Manners had always placed confidence in him, and therefore put the poor boy under his charge. When the grain was gathered in at the harvest, the overseer scored down the number of bushels, and when it was afterwards sold, Felix did so, by his orders; there were a hundred bushels less than the first count.

"'How is this, Felix?' said he, ' you have either miscounted the quantity or you have stolen a hundred bushels. I shall inform Mrs. Manners of the hypocrite who thus abuses her goodness, for many persons saw the grain first measured, and I have observed you frequently carrying away bundles.'

"It was in vain for Felix to protest his innocence; the overseer was determined to ruin him, and thus get quit of one whom he feared would sooner or later witness against him.

"Mrs. Manners had some months before lost a diamond breastpin, and as she had no reason to suspect any one about the house of stealing it, supposed she had lost it while walking. Felix was summoned before her to answer the accusation of his enemy, who stated that there could be no doubt of his guilt, as he had found a small sack with Mrs. Truely's name on it, behind his trunk, containing the refuse of wheat; and that his wife had also found the diamond pin in his waistcoat while washing it.

"Felix Truely went up to Mrs. Manners and said: 'It is in vain for me to assert my innocence; I leave my cause in the hands of God; I have never wilfully offended him, and he will one day show forth who is the guilty one. Do with me what you please; I only grieve for my poor mother, whose heart will be broken at the thought of her son being called a criminal—for *she* will never believe me guilty of robbing my benefactress. May God comfort my poor parent in the bitter hour of trial.'

"He stood calm and dignified. Mrs. Manners burst into tears—told him to return to his mother—that she could not resolve to bring him to justice—besought him to repent ere it was too late, and begged him to go at once, for she had truly loved him.

"The overseer remarked that it was

not very prudent to let such a delin-
quent go unpunished.

"'It is my intention to give him time
to repent,' said she, 'on account of his
youth; and I can yet hardly understand
how one who had never before given
me any reason to think evil of him,
should thus, all at once, fall.'

"The man muttered something about
hypocrites, but she remained firm to her
decision. Felix Manners looked first at
his poor friend and then at his accuser,
and the malicious exultation of the latter was not lost upon him.

"It was a sad meeting that night
between the poor mother and son. 'I
know you are not guilty, my dear child,
and we must bow with resignation to
the will of God,' said Mrs. Truely; and
Felix took his crucifix and prayed, 'Oh,
my beloved Redeemer! strengthen thy

poor child and enable him to bear igno-
miny for the love of Thee !'

"After the departure of the poor boy
Felix Manners became sad and solitary;
He did not believe him guilty, for how
could a mere child carry away a hundred bushels of wheat in a small sack;
more particularly as his mother always
kept the key of the granary, and Felix
had never been entrusted with it, nor
had she ever missed it from her bunch
of keys. Felix also had an indistinct
remembrance that on the day his mother
had missed the breastpin he had seen
confusion in the manner of the overseer's
daughter, (who was chambermaid,) when
he came suddenly into his mother's room,
and he felt convinced that his poor friend
was the victim of a vile plot, which he
was determined to unfold, if possible.

" The overseer spread the story about;

and Felix Truely could get no employment. George Ellis, (the boy who had intended to rob him at the bridge,) came and offered to share his fortunes with him. He had indeed reformed, and Mrs. Manners had secured him plenty of work, and the esteem of those who had formerly despised him. But Felix would not deprive him of his earnings, if he could earn bread for his poor parent he cared not for himself; yet though George could not get him to accept anything for himself, he could not prevent him from privately placing baskets of provisions in the cottage window, for the repentant boy was anxious to repair his former faults towards Felix.

One evening as Felix Manners was walking in one of his mother's fields, a paper lying in the long grass caught his eye, he carelessly picked it up, and found it to be a letter addressed to the wife of the overseer, and he recognized his handwriting. He had gone to a distant city some days before on urgent business. As Felix held the letter undecided what to do with it, the words *Felix* and *wheat* caught his attention, (for the letter was open,) and at that moment the person to whom it was addressed came running in great agitation, and seeing the fatal letter open in his hand, exclaimed, 'Have you *dared* to read my letter?'

" 'I have not read it—but you forget to whom you are speaking.'

" ' Give it to me, or I will make you.'

" 'I shall not,' said Felix, quietly; for he saw that it contained something relating to the late affair. She darted at him with furious looks, but he flew away like a lapwing, and stopped not until he found himself at his mother's side. He told his story, and Mrs. Manners felt justified in seeing the contents of the letter and sent for witnesses to approve her conduct. It was as follows:

"'*Dear Wife:*—I have sold the hundred bushels of wheat at a great profit, and shall bring home a nice sum, and we can then buy the carriage you want so much. I have besides got a good bargain for the ox that we made the mistress believe was dead—and but for that pest, Felix, I could have sold the breastpin for nearly its value; but you know I had to give it up in order to criminate that miserable ploughboy, who wanted to be a gentleman over his betters. I shall be home in two days, and in the meantime you must spread about that you have received a legacy. Burn this, &c.'

" 'Dear Felix!' exclaimed Mrs. Manners, 'how have we wronged you—let us hasten to repair the injurious treatment he has received from us.'

"Before the overseer could be informed by his wife, he was arrested and placed in the county jail to await his trial. Mrs. Manners proceeded to the cottage, asked pardon for her great injustice; took the mother and son home, and adopted them both into her house and heart.

"It was again St. Felix's day, and the two youths knelt at the altar to receive, for the first time, the Bread of Life. Who can paint the transports of those souls with whom the Lord of heaven and earth deigns to come and take up his abode? 'I have found my Beloved—I hold him, and will not let him go until he shall bless me.'

"Happiness beamed in the faces of those two boys; their secret prayers and the pure offerings of their hearts were registered on high. George Ellis, too, was there, and was received into the bosom of that Church from which he had so long strayed. He was employed by Mrs. Manners and afterwards became her steward, which office he filled with capability and faithfulness.

"Fifteen years had passed, and two priests were seen one day kneeling before two graves in the village cemetery, absorbed in prayer. They rose and pursued their way through the romantic pathway, before spoken of, and paused before the ruins of a cottage.

"'Blessed be the memory of my departed mother!' exclaimed the elder; 'for by her piety and prayers God preserved me from the snares of the enemy.

You remember the prayer we offered on the day of our first communion,' said he, addressing his companion.

"'Yes, my brother,' was the reply; 'and God has indeed heard those prayers, since it has pleased him to call us to consecrate ourselves to his service. To-morrow is our Annual Festival, and what happiness will be ours to officiate at that altar where we 'first offered ourselves to God.'

"You will easily perceive, my dear children, that these two servants of God were Felix Manners and Felix Truely. They never came again—but for many years St. Felix's day was a day of rejoicing amongst the youth of the village.

Sixth Evening.

Good and Bad Example.

ON what subject are you all discoursing so earnestly?" asked Miss Onslow, as she entered the room where her pupils were assembled.

"We are speaking of good and bad example," replied one of the oldest girls; "and Ann Darby has just said that it only applies to grown persons, for nobody takes notice of the example of children. I was going to show her she is wrong, by relating that, yesterday mamma desired me not to go into the garden while the grass was wet,

(109)

but I paid no attention to her orders and went. Mamma was much displeased with me, not only because I had dis-obeyed her, but because my little brother followed my example and is sick to-day in consequence. Now, did not that ex-ample cause my brother to be disobe-dient and to suffer also besides?"

"But your brother did not know you were forbidden to go, and therefore was not disobedient," persisted Ann.

"Yes, he did know it, and thought mamma quite unkind to keep us in the house. But even had he not known it, though he would not have been disobe-dient, yet my example caused him a sick-ness he might not otherwise have had. Am I not right?" continued she, turn-ing to her teacher.

"Certainly, my love," you were the cause of both; but as you have had the courage openly to speak of your fault,

by which you not only displeased your
mamma but offended God, I trust you
will never again commit it. When
children have arrived at the age of reason, that is, when they are old enough
to know right from wrong, then they
become bound to set a good example.
I remember that when I was a child,
my mother one morning desired me to
return home immediately after school.
I promised, but seeing some pretty butterflies in a field near the school, I asked
one of my companions to stay and help
me catch them. She said that her sister
did not seem quite well when she left
home and she was required to hasten
back. I replied that it would only be a
few minutes more, and so insisted that
at last she complied. We spent more
than two hours and caught one poor
butterfly. When I returned home my
mother pointed out the faults I had com-

mitted through disobedience and bad
example. But this was not all. My
companion found her sister very ill—
there had been nobody to go for the
physician during her absence, and, in
consequence, the child had a painful
and protracted illness, from which she
never entirely recovered—so my bad
example produced a sad result that I
had not anticipated and which I have
never forgotten or ceased to lament."

The teacher paused in great emotion.
After awhile she continued: "I will
relate the history of a little girl, which
will prove to you the importance of
example at every age:"

"Susan was the daughter of Martin,
a poor laborer, who worked very indus-
triously to support his family, and lived
as a pious and sincere Christian. His
wife, who was named Catharine, followed his bright example, and taught

her children to love God from their
earliest years. . At the time my story
begins they had seen all their loved ones
die, except Susan, who was remarkable
for her piety. At four years old she
might be seen in the church with her
little hands clasped together, her eyes
fixed on 'the Crucifix or on a statue of
the Blessed Virgin, and not a sound or
movement on her part disturbed the
attention of those who were there assembled. Such, my dear children, should
be the conduct of all, both old and
young, who enter the Holy Temple of
God. Even at that tender age she was
the means of converting a young woman, who sometimes went to that church,
but whose attention was always taken ·
up with gazing at those who entered, or
in whispering to some companion as
irreverent as herself; who never knelt
devoutly during the August Sacrifice of

the Mass, when our Divine Redeemer
is present on the altar, at the words pronounced by the priests to whom He has
given this power; whose conduct, in
short, was so offensive to God and so
greatly annoyed those who came there
really to pray, that Susan, being one
day placed near her, looked in her face,
with eyes streaming with tears, and
whispered, "God is looking at us—do
not make Him angry." When they left
the church that young woman followed
and asked her to pray for her. The
prayers and beautiful example of the
child converted her, as she has often
since assured me, and she afterwards
became as remarkable for her piety as
she had before been the contrary.

"Susan was about twelve years old
when Martin received a letter from his
brother's daughter, informing him of the
death of her father, and begging him to

receive her, as she was left entirely des-
titute. He sent for and received her
with affection. She was ten years old;
had been brought up in idleness, and
knew little or nothing. She was very
careless about her religious duties, and
never said her prayers or even desired
to attend Mass.

" 'I cannot understand how you can
be happy when you do not say your
prayers, or do anything that the church
requires,' said Susan to her one day.

" 'Oh! my father did not bother himself about such things,' she replied, 'and
never taught me any such practices—we
had plenty whilst we lived, and what
more is necessary in this world? I shall
soon be able to get enough without my
uncle's help, or having to live so very
saint-like.' So saying with a sneer she
left the good Susan. How many are
like poor Rose, thinking of nothing but

what they can gain in this world, without remembering that God will require something of them — for the things gained in this world alone are only for his enemy.

"Susan was much grieved to see Rose so careless of her salvation, and begged her to pause and reflect, and her uncle and aunt used every means to bring her to a sense of her duty, but in vain.

"One day Susan requested her to assist in finishing some plain sewing which she had promised to take home the next morning. Rose refused, became very angry, and used injurious words. The pious girl made no reply, and, after saying her prayers, sat up nearly all night to complete her task. At an early hour she went to Mass, and then proceeded to the house of the lady—delivered her work, and received payment. As she returned home she met Rose, who seemed confused, and made some trifling excuse to leave her. Whilst she was preparing the breakfast, two men entered, and inquired for her cousin. They were yet speaking when Rose entered by the back door, and seeing them would have fled. They produced a warrant accusing her of stealing some valuable lace from a shop, and in spite of her denial and tears, she was taken to jail.

"Susan received permission to visit her; she consoled her, wept with her, and prayed for her, and talked so beautifully of the danger she was in of losing her soul, and of being confined eternally to a prison far more horrible than that she was now condemned to, and of the bliss of heaven reserved for those that serve God, that at last the hitherto obdurate and impenitent girl knelt and prayed for pardon for her sins. She was at length released and returned to her uncle's house. She fell into many of her former faults, but the untiring charity, patience, piety, and constant good example of Susan were finally rewarded by her amendment, and she learned to know, love and serve God.

"Soon afterwards Susan fell into an alarming illness, from which she never recovered. She called Rose to her, and begged her to supply her place towards her parents. The reformed girl promised and kept her word; and blessed her dying cousin for the good example she had set her and which had saved her. She afterwards, by her good conduct, reclaimed a young girl who had become quite wicked by listening to her bad advice and following her evil example."

"Will you now say, my dear children, that the good or bad example of children is of no importance?"

"No, indeed," replied Ann; "and I will endeavor to imitate Susan."

At this moment Mrs. Grenville appeared. She was eagerly welcomed by the children, to whom she had promised to relate a story on devotion to the Blessed Virgin, as a fitting close to the last of the "Cottage Evenings." The story was as follows:

"In a small village, beautfully situated on the banks of a river, one cottage might be distinguished from the rest by its air of neatness, the roses that clustered over its porch, and the little garden attached to it. It was inhabited by old Nannie Dale and her grand-daughter Mary. The latter was about twelve years of age and a model of filial piety. She attended to the slightest wants of her aged and infirm relative, kept the cottage so clean, the little garden so full of sweet flowers, and clear of weeds, and was always so

early at church that she was called 'the
pride of the village'—a name which
alarmed her humility. She was as mo-
dest and retiring as the violet, and so
full of benevolence, that she shared her
scanty meals with those less fortunate
than herself. Her sister Josephine (some
years older) lived with a lady in the
neighborhood, in the capacity of lady's
maid. She was as remarkable for her
want of piety and humility as Mary was
for both. The only thing she had not
discarded was a medal of our Lady, which
she had promised her dying mother always to wear, and to recite the prayer on
it—which promise she kept. She seldom
saw Mary, for she feared her gentle re-
proofs.

It was the custom of the village girls
to crown a queen, chosen by lot, on the
first day of every May. They assembled
for this purpose in the park of Mr. Good-
all, who loved to witness their innocent
festivity, and who also provided a suit-
able entertainment, laid out under the
magnificent oak trees, which had flour-

ished there for a century. A beautiful temple had also been erected by him and dedicated to the Blessed Virgin Mary; it was adorned by a marble statue, as large as life, of our Holy Mother. It was there they crowned the queen elect, who was required at the same time to select one of the favorite virtues of the Holy Queen under whose auspices she was crowned, to practice during the year, and at the succeeding annual festival to give an account of her observance of it, and if she had failed she was never re-elected. This rule was productive of much good, for she who was considered as too bad to be nominated a second time, was in a manner under disgrace.

"'Who do you think will be Queen?' said Ellen Parr to Mary, as they sat together at the cottage window on the eve of May.

"'I know whom I would choose,' she replied, 'but grandmamma is so feeble that I do not think I shall be there.'

"The morn had scarcely smiled in the

east, when groups of joyous girls had assembled in the park; their white dresses and ribbons formed a pretty contrast to the dark trees, hung with festoons of roses. The Ave Maria ascended in melodious accents, but all missed the sweet accents of Mary; she was yet absent. They next proceeded to nominate the Queen, and, by a vote almost unanimous, Mary was elected. They sent to tell her, and she came, but in sadness, for her grandparent was rapidly declining; but, in obedience to her wishes, she left her to the care of Mrs. Parr.

"'Oh, Mary!' said Ellen, running to meet her, 'I am so glad that you are Queen; come, we are waiting to crown you.'

"Mary knelt, and a beautiful wreath of white roses and lily of the valley was placed on her her head by Ellen, who said, 'these blossoms will soon fade, but our love for our May Queen, never.'

"The Queen arose, and whilst tears of mingled emotions coursed down her cheeks, she replied, 'I thank you, my friends and companions, for this mark of love and preference; but there is one whom we should love and prefer still more. I therefore use the usual privilege granted of resigning my crown to another, and I place it where you will best love to see it.'

"She then covered the brow of the statue with the sweet offering. A murmur of approbation ran through the crowd, and, kneeling, they chanted the Litany. As the last notes died away, Mary's prayer was heard: 'Oh! blessed Mother and Queen, may I soon see thee crowned in heaven.'

"'And pray,' said Josephine, who had witnessed the ceremony and heard her prayer, but who had not even asked for her grandmother, 'why could you not have crowned me instead of that old statue? Indeed, I fully expected to be Queen.'

"Mary answered in a tone of gentle reproof; 'If you deem yourself more worthy than the Queen of heaven to whom I have made the offering, take the wreath from her brow,' but Josephine turned away angry and abashed.

"The party had just commenced partaking of strawberries and cream, with other danties, when Mary was sent for to attend her dying parent—she entreated her sister to go with her, but in vain —she hated such melancholy scenes.

"'I am about to leave you, dear child,' said old Nannie, as her grandchild approached, 'and I have yet a duty to perform. I bequeath you to the care of Mrs. Parr, who will be a mother to you, all the little I possess is yours. Love God with your whole heart, detest sin as the only real evil, be a faithful follower of the cross, devote yourself to the blessed Mother of God, and your Mayday prayer will be heard.' She kissed her loved one, then her crucifix, and was at rest.

"The summer passed away—fresh flowers constantly graced the brow of the statue, yet none saw who placed them there. Poor Mary was gentle, loving, and unwearied in serving all, but it was evident that her strength gradually decreased, and that her thoughts were not of this world. She was often missed, and generally found in the May temple. One day during the winter she was heard to exclaim—'How I sigh for May day.'

"'Do you expect to be again crowned?' said Ellen smiling.

"'No, but I desire to see the Queen of May,' she replied.

"Her companion understood her, and wept, for she saw her passing away as rapidly as the snow melts under the beams of a mid-day sun. She never spoke of her sister, who had not changed her evil ways, but they heard her pronounce her name when praying in the temple. Ellen now saw May day approaching with a saddened heart.

"It came at length in sunshine and beauty. The villagers assembled as formerly, and after reciting morning prayers, they said as usual the Ave Maria. On arriving at the temple, they found in the hand of the statue a scroll, with the words, 'Our Queen reigns for ever!' and

Mary lying at its feet. They raised her, she was dead. Her prayer had been heard. A death-like silence prevailed for a moment at this sight—then with a shrill cry Josephine rushed forward and embraced the corpse of the beautiful and blest. 'Gone,' said she, 'gone to bliss, and I—what am I? Speak to me, Mary, and say I shall be forgiven.'

"Three years passed away, and the priest was standing at the death bed of the contrite Josephine. She saw the faint streaks of early dawn through the lattice, and said, 'Father, is not this May day? I come—I come;'—and the soul of the redeemed winged its flight to another habitation. The villagers erected a monument which may still be seen, on which the words: 'To our beloved Mary and Josephine Dale,' were inscribed."

THE END.